HOW DO WE KNOW

DINOSAURS EXISTED?

MIKE BENTON

RSVP

RAINTREE STECK-VAUGHN
P U B L I S H E R S
The Steck-Vaughn Company

Austin, Texas

Published by Raintree Steck-Vaughn Publishers, an imprint of
Steck-Vaughn Company

Commissioning Editor: Thomas Keegan
Designer: Neville Graham
Editors: Kate Scarborough and Maurice J. Sabean
Illustrators: John Butler and Alan Male

Library of Congress Cataloging-in-Publication Data

Benton, M. J. (Michael J.)
   Dinosaurs existed? / Mike Benton.
     p.   cm.—(How do we know)
   Includes index.
   ISBN 0-8114-3878-3
   1. Dinosaurs—Juvenile literature. [1. Dinosaurs.] I. Title.
II. Title: How do we know dinosaurs existed?   III. Series.
QE862.D5B457   1995
567.9′1—dc20
                                                94–16252
                                                 CIP
                                                   AC

Printed and bound in Hong Kong

1 2 3 4 5 6 7 8 9 0 HK 99 98 97 96 95 94

The words in boldface type are explained in the glossary.

Contents

HOW DO WE KNOW
About Dinosaurs?

Dinosaurs were big, and they lived a long time ago. There were at least twenty different kinds of dinosaurs, and they were fierce, brainless animals. They died out because they were hopeless failures.

These are the kinds of ideas that many people have about dinosaurs, and yet they are mainly wrong. Many dinosaurs were indeed big, but there were also small ones. Dinosaurs were in fact one of the most successful groups of animals of all time: they ruled the Earth for over 150 million years. They did indeed live a long time ago—long before the first humans appeared on Earth.

And there were many different species of dinosaurs. Since the first discoveries of dinosaurs, paleontologists (the scientists who study fossils) have named about 1,000 species of dinosaurs from all continents on the Earth. Every year, another ten species are discovered.

Brachiosaurus
The largest well-known dinosaur. Evidence of *Brachiosaurus* has been found in Tanzania (Africa) and in North America. It reached a length of 74 feet (22.5 m) and stood as tall as a three-story building. It was a giant plant-eater.

Plateosaurus
One of the first large dinosaurs, *Plateosaurus* was a plant-eater. Some specimens were up to 26 feet (8 m) long, but many were smaller. *Plateosaurus* used its strong hands to gather leaves from tall trees.

Compsognathus
A small, rare dinosaur known from only a couple of specimens found in Germany and France. *Compsognathus*, at 2 feet (0.6 m) long, was one of the smallest dinosaurs.

Stegosaurus
One of the most famous plant-eating dinosaurs of North America. *Stegosaurus* was up to 24.5 feet (7.5 m) long and had a double row of bony plates down the middle of its back. These may have been for defense or for temperature control.

Triceratops
A large 29.5-foot- (9-m-) long plant-eater found in North America. Its long horns may have been used in fighting, and the heavy bony plate at the back of the skull may have helped protect the neck.

Pteranodon
Not a dinosaur, but a pterosaur, or flying reptile of North America. It had a wingspan of 30 feet (7 m), larger than any bird and more like a hang glider.

Tyrannosaurus
The most famous dinosaur. *Tyrannosaurus* of North America fed on plant-eating dinosaurs. At 46 feet (14 m) long, and with an open mouth of nearly 3 feet (1 m), *Tyrannosaurus* was a fearsome predator.

DINOSAUR CLASSIFICATION

All dinosaurs are related to each other. They arose from a single **ancestor** about 230 million years ago. About 5 million years later, the Dinosauria split into two major groups. The saurischians include all the meat-eaters and the long-necked plant-eaters. The ornithischians were all plant-eaters. The two groups differ in the arrangement of the three large bones of the hip.

In saurischians, the bones point in three directions.

In ornithischians, the lower front bone has swung back.

HOW DO WE KNOW

Dinosaurs Existed?

Dinosaurs were first found hundreds of years ago. But these extinct giants have only really been known for less than 200 years. The first dinosaur was named in 1824, and since then, hundreds of different species have been discovered in all parts of the world. The story began in Great Britain and Germany, but by 1870, the most exciting dinosaur discoveries were coming from North America. After that, the search for dinosaurs spread worldwide, and dozens of huge skeletons came to light in the remotest parts of the world. The search still goes on today. The latest finds have come from Antarctica.

THE FIRST DINOSAUR

The first dinosaur that we know about was shown in a book about the natural history of Oxfordshire, England, in 1677. A professor at Oxford University wrote about all the strange rocks that had been sent to him, one of which he recognized as a giant bone. He knew it was from the lower end of a thighbone and that it was too big to have come from an elephant. In the end, he thought it came from a giant man or woman!

We now know that this bone came from the meat-eating dinosaur *Megalosaurus*. In fact, *Megalosaurus* was the first dinosaur ever to be given a name. Other bones had been found over the years, and Professor William Buckland, also of Oxford University, collected them together, and gave the dinosaur a name in 1824. *Megalosaurus* means "big lizard," which is just what he thought it was. Buckland thought that *Megalosaurus* was a huge meat-eating lizard, up to 200 feet (60 m) long!

Megalosaurus

Megalosaurus (shown below) is now known to have been a large, two-legged meat-eating theropod. More complete skeletons have come to light since 1824, and these show much more detail than Buckland could ever have known. Buckland had only a bit of a jawbone and some other odds and ends from the skeleton to work with.

A thighbone
The first dinosaur bone ever to be found! This is the lower end of a *Megalosaurus* thighbone, from just above the knee.

Professor Buckland
William Buckland (1784–1856) was professor of geology at Oxford University and also dean of Christ Church Cathedral there. He was famous not only for studying dinosaurs, but he was also one of the first people to realize that there had been a great Ice Age in a late phase of Earth's history.

IGUANA TOOTH

The second dinosaur to be named was *Iguanodon*, a plant-eating dinosaur. Some teeth had been found in Sussex, England, in 1822, and other bones soon were found. A local geologist, Gideon Mantell, saw that the teeth came from a plant-eater, and he thought it was another giant lizard. *Iguanodon* means "iguana tooth," since the fossil teeth look a little like the teeth of the modern plant-eating lizards, the iguanas.

Jawbone
Fragment of the jawbone of *Megalosaurus* showing the large meat-eating teeth: one large tooth stands up on the edge.

Gideon Mantell

Gideon Mantell (1790–1852) was a physician in England, and also a renowned amateur geologist in his spare time. He would hunt for fossils while out on his medical visiting rounds. He wrote some very popular books about geology, which sold thousands of copies, and he was one of the first people to make fossil-collecting popular as a hobby. He reported several new dinosaurs from the south of England.

GREAT REPTILES

By 1842, several more dinosaurs had been named from bones discovered in England and in Germany. In that year, Richard Owen, professor of anatomy at the Royal College of Surgeons in London, invented the name *dinosaur*, which means "terrible reptile." He thought the dinosaurs were not lizards at all, but great, rhinoceroslike reptiles. His dinosaur models can still be seen in Crystal Palace park in south London.

Richard Owen

COMPLETE SKELETONS

New finds from North America changed everyone's ideas about the dinosaurs. These new specimens were whole skeletons, not just bits and pieces. One of the first skeletons from North America was of *Hadrosaurus*, a duckbilled dinosaur.

From 1870 to 1900, hundreds of dinosaur skeletons were dug up in the West during the time of the "bone wars." Two paleontologists, Othniel Marsh of Yale University and Edward Cope of Philadelphia, had a race to find more new kinds of dinosaurs than the other. They hated each other, and each spent thousands of dollars to pay workmen to dig as fast as they could.

Hadrosaur skeleton

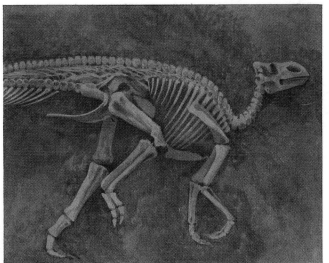

ALL OVER THE WORLD

In this century, the search for dinosaurs has gone farther afield. Great discoveries have been made in Africa, South America, Mongolia, China, Australia, and India. Until 1987, only the frozen wastes of Antarctica had never produced a dinosaur. Since then, three or more dinosaur skeletons have been found there.

Ankylosaurus
An armored dinosaur, a group found all over the world

HOW DO WE KNOW
Where to Find Dinosaurs?

Dinosaurs have been found in all parts of the world, from New York to London, from Russia to Australia, and from Alaska to Antarctica. Most dinosaurs have been found in remote places, a long way from civilization, often in badlands. Badlands are often dry and very little can grow, but they are good lands for finding dinosaurs, because the bare rock is exposed at the surface, and the wind and rain wash away the soil and rock. This makes it easy to find bones.

However, some discoveries have been made in areas not far from large cities. For example, evidence of large dinosaurs has been found in regions that are now populated, such as Connecticut. The best prospect for new finds is to go to unexplored parts of the world where rocks the right age are exposed.

The Badlands of South Dakota
Fossil bones were first found here around 1850. Since then, many hundreds of skeletons have been dug up and sent to museums all over the United States and other countries. Desertlike plants grow on top of the plain, and rainwater has cut out deep **gulleys** through the earth and rock.

1. Prospecting
Dinosaur hunters look for bones by searching back and forth in badlands for days on end. When they find some good pieces of bone washed downstream, they follow them back to the source and start to dig.

2. Digging
The overburden (rock lying over the skeleton) is removed with picks and shovels, and sometimes even with backhoes and pneumatic drills. The dinosaur hunters are much more careful when they get down to the bones!

3. Mapping
The rock is removed carefully from the skeleton using small hand tools. It is important to make a detailed map of how the skeleton is lying in the rock and to take photographs all the time so that it will be easier to put the skeleton back together again in the lab.

4. Plastering
The bones are carefully cleared and covered with sackcloth soaked in plaster. Layers of plaster set hard and make a very strong package. The packaged bones are carefully removed and loaded up for the trip back to the museum laboratory.

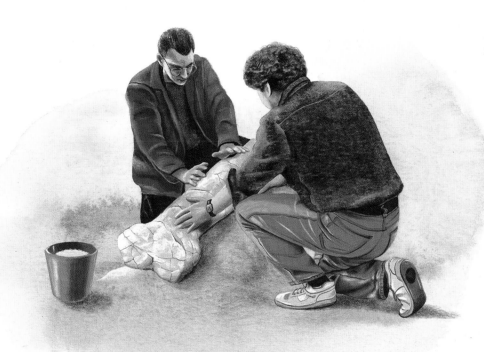

AT THE MUSEUM
In the museum, the bones have to be taken out of their plaster coverings, cleaned up, and then strengthened. The bones may be big, but they are often crumbly. Special glues are used to soak into the **porous** bone and to hold broken pieces together.

Framing
If a skeleton is mounted for display, it must be held up on a metal or fiberglass frame.

Putting it together
Putting a dinosaur skeleton together is like solving a **three-dimensional** jigsaw puzzle. The shape of the bones tells the scientists what they are. Missing bones can be made in plaster.

How to Reconstruct Dinosaurs?

The main job of the paleontologist (a scientist who studies dinosaurs and other fossil animals and plants) is to make the ancient world come to life. How does the paleontologist make a living animal from a pile of old bones? Can you believe the pictures, stories, and movies about dinosaurs, or is it all just a scientist's imagination? It is actually possible to learn a great deal from dinosaur bones, from other fossils of plants and animals, and even from the rocks in which the fossils are found. But the first and most important evidence comes from a very detailed look at the dinosaur bones.

LOOKING AT BONES

When the bones have been cleaned up and strengthened, they are laid out in the lab so that they can be identified. It may be possible to fit some of them together, like the separate bones of the backbone (the vertebrae), which lock together closely. The paleontologists will try to identify the dinosaur by comparing their newly discovered bones with **specimens** found before, and with drawings of bones that have been published in scientific journals.

PUTTING FLESH ON THE BONES

The fossils are only the hard parts of the dinosaur, its skeleton. How can a paleontologist put the flesh back on as well? Flesh, the soft parts of an animal's body, is mainly muscle. Muscles are there to make parts of the body move, and they are all attached to bones at each end. Ancient dinosaur bones give clues about dinosaur flesh. There are often clear marks where the muscles used to be.

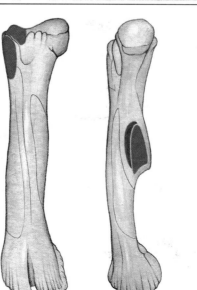
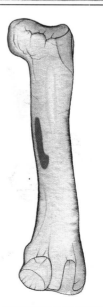

Shaded areas are where muscles attach.

TESTING JOINTS

How much could a dinosaur bend its arm, leg, or neck? If the bones are well preserved, the paleontologist can fit the joints together and find out. The bones of the hip, knee, and ankle joints, for example, can show exactly how a dinosaur moved its hind leg. Here are three different joints that allow a varying amount of movement.

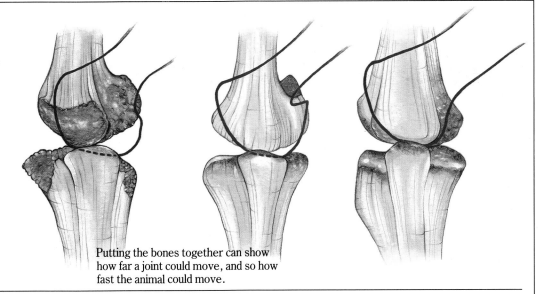

Putting the bones together can show how far a joint could move, and so how fast the animal could move.

HOW HEAVY?

Some of the long-necked, plant-eating dinosaurs were the biggest land animals of all time. But how big were they? Paleontologists can figure out how heavy a dinosaur was if they make a detailed model of the animal with its flesh. The heaviest ones, like *Brachiosaurus*, could reach 50 tons. If a dinosaur had been heavier than 100 tons or so, its legs would have been so fat that it could not have walked!

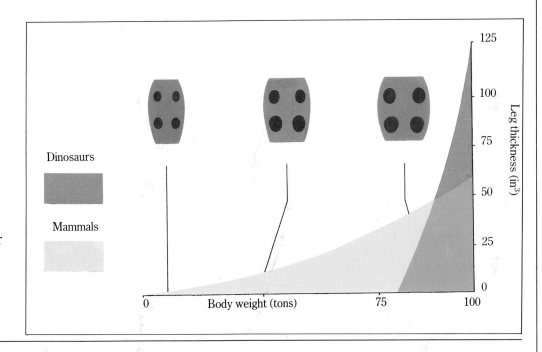

Dinosaurs

Mammals

Leg thickness (in³)

Body weight (tons)

MUSCLES

The final piece of evidence is to look at modern animals. Paleontologists might compare the leg of a dinosaur with that of a crocodile or a bird to see where the muscles were located. All backboned animals have roughly the same muscles, and it is likely that dinosaurs had these muscles also. Our biceps muscle bends our arm up, and it is just the same in a gorilla, a lizard, and a dinosaur.

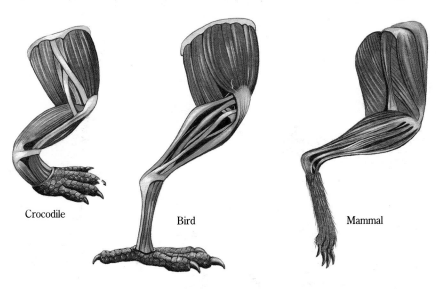

Crocodile

Bird

Mammal

How Dinosaurs Moved?

When the muscles have been added to a dinosaur skeleton, can we understand any more about how that dinosaur lived? How fast could it run, what did it eat, what noises did it make, what color was it? These questions are tackled later in the book. But first, the whole animal has to be understood. And a clear model or picture has to be made to show the living dinosaur in a setting that includes other animals and plants that it saw when it walked around millions of years ago.

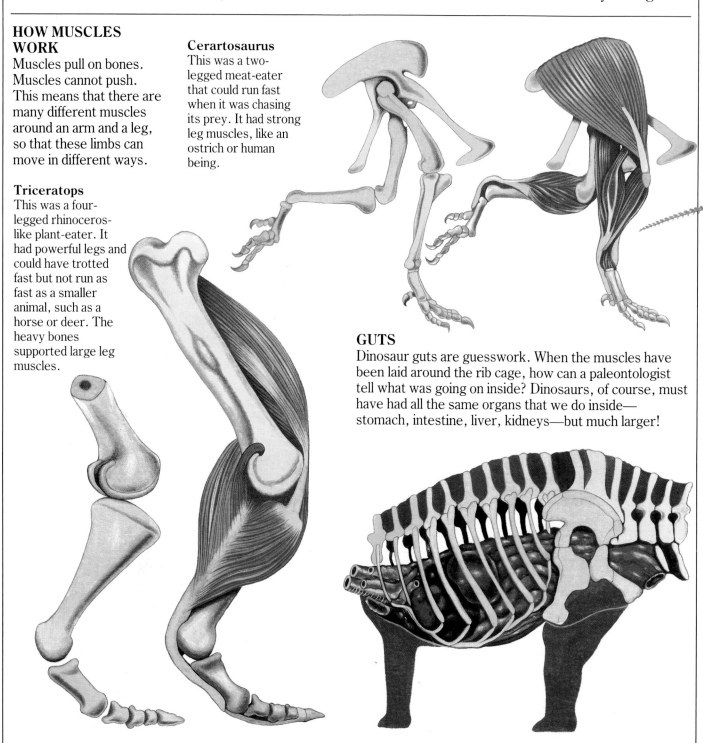

HOW MUSCLES WORK

Muscles pull on bones. Muscles cannot push. This means that there are many different muscles around an arm and a leg, so that these limbs can move in different ways.

Triceratops

This was a four-legged rhinoceros-like plant-eater. It had powerful legs and could have trotted fast but not run as fast as a smaller animal, such as a horse or deer. The heavy bones supported large leg muscles.

Cerartosaurus

This was a two-legged meat-eater that could run fast when it was chasing its prey. It had strong leg muscles, like an ostrich or human being.

GUTS

Dinosaur guts are guesswork. When the muscles have been laid around the rib cage, how can a paleontologist tell what was going on inside? Dinosaurs, of course, must have had all the same organs that we do inside—stomach, intestine, liver, kidneys—but much larger!

PUTTING IT ALL TOGETHER

The guts may be guesswork, but the flesh and bones are not. From a fairly complete skeleton, paleontologists can be quite sure about the shape of a dinosaur and about its muscles.

Bones

The skeleton is strung together, and all the joints are tested carefully. The pose of the body is based on the close study of the joints and on comparisons with large living animals.

Muscles

The muscles are laid on layer by layer after a study of muscle scars on the bones. The scars tell us where the muscles attached and roughly how large they were.

Skin

The other soft parts are more difficult to reconstruct. The skin is then laid over the whole body. But what color was the skin?

MAKING A MODEL

Models of reconstructed dinosaurs are made for display in museums. The models are made smaller than the real thing, of course, and they may take weeks of careful scientific study and artistic work to put together. Sometimes these detailed models may be made of plastic so that everyone can buy one. Of course, most plastic dinosaur models are not very accurate!

You can measure the volume of a model dinosaur by filling a glass full of water. Lower the dinosaur into the glass and catch the water that spills over the edge. The weight of this water will give you the volume of the dinosaur. You can use this to compare the relative size of your model to a real dinosaur.

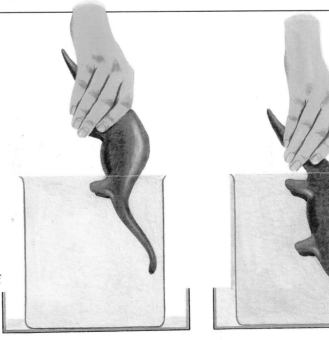

13

HOW DO WE KNOW
What Color They Were?

No one has ever found a fossil that shows the color of a dinosaur. Surprisingly, there are quite a few specimens of dinosaur skin, or at least molds of the skin pressed into the rock beside a skeleton. Usually, of course, the skin and flesh rot away completely. But, in some cases, dinosaurs seem to have been **mummified**, because the soft parts dried out under the hot sun, and the whole body was buried. Eventually, the flesh rotted away, but an impression of the skin may survive. These skin fossils show that most dinosaurs had scales of some kind. Many dinosaurs also had very thick plates of bone set into their skin, as crocodiles do today, to give protection.

Can we know?
What color were the big sauropods, such as *Apatosaurus*? Were they green, brown, blue, purple with orange spots? We shall never know.

What color were they?
Many scientists suspect that dinosaurs were brightly colored like their closest living relatives, birds and lizards.

14

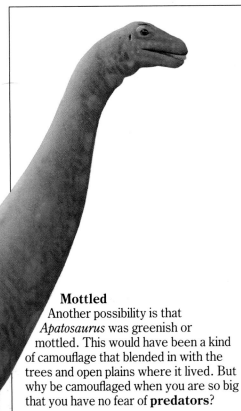

Mottled

Another possibility is that *Apatosaurus* was greenish or mottled. This would have been a kind of camouflage that blended in with the trees and open plains where it lived. But why be camouflaged when you are so big that you have no fear of **predators**?

WHY ARE ANIMALS COLORED?

Camouflage

Many animals today are camouflaged. Their colors match the background and make them hard to see. This can be useful for plant-eaters or meat-eaters, since it allows them to hide.

Warning

Some animals have warning colors. Some snakes and lizards, for example, are colored with bright reds, yellows, and blacks. This tells predators "keep away, I bite."

Temperature control

Color may be involved in temperature control. In hot climates, many large animals are dull gray or brown. These colors may not absorb as much heat from the sun as darker colors. This may have been true also of the larger dinosaurs.

Advertising

Color may also be used to send messages to other animals of the same species. Many male birds are brightly colored as a kind of advertisement to the females. The colors say, "look how handsome and smart I am. I will be a good father for your children."

How Long Ago They Lived?

The Earth is very old. It formed about 4.6 billion years ago. The first living things appeared about 3.5 billion years ago. Humans only came on the scene about 5 million years ago. How do paleontologists know this? Is it just guesswork? The answers come from geologists, scientists who study the history of the Earth. They can figure out these ages from the rocks. There are great thicknesses of rocks that can be seen in **quarries**, in cliffs, and even in deep holes drilled through the Earth's crust. The order of the layers of rocks, the fossils found in the rocks, and **radioactive elements** can all give evidence of age.

DATING THE FOSSILS

When geologists look at the order of the rocks, from very old ones to younger ones, they can see that the fossils are in some kind of order, too. The oldest rocks have no fossils. As the fossils become younger, they contain simple single-celled creatures, then sponges and corals, then shellfish, then fish, and so on.

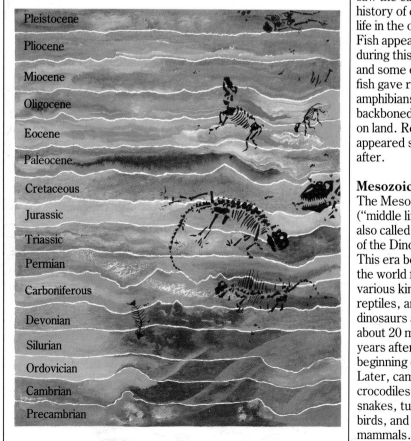

Pleistocene
Pliocene
Miocene
Oligocene
Eocene
Paleocene
Cretaceous
Jurassic
Triassic
Permian
Carboniferous
Devonian
Silurian
Ordovician
Cambrian
Precambrian

A SWEEP OF TIME

The diagram below shows the great sweep of geological time, running from the origin of the Earth to the present day. Dinosaurs appeared late in the story but still long, long before the first humans.

PALEOZOIC 570–245 million years ago

250 million years ago

205 million years ago

13 mill years

Paleozoic

The Paleozoic ("ancient life") Era saw the early history of complex life in the oceans. Fish appeared early during this time, and some of these fish gave rise to amphibians, the first backboned animals on land. Reptiles appeared soon after.

Mesozoic

The Mesozoic ("middle life") Era is also called the Age of the Dinosaurs. This era began with the world full of various kinds of reptiles, and the dinosaurs arose about 20 million years after the beginning of the era. Later, came the crocodiles, lizards, snakes, turtles, birds, and mammals.

Cenozoic

The Cenozoic ("recent life") Era began after the great extinction of the dinosaurs and of many other Mesozoic groups on land and in the ocean. The Earth became dominated by mammals on land. The latest major mammal group to appear were humans, at almost 5 million years ago.

HOW ANIMALS TURN TO STONE

Fossils are the remains of plants and animals that once lived. Usually, fossils are the hard parts of those ancient creatures, like bones or shells, with all the spaces filled with rock. In bone there are many internal cavities that contain blood vessels, **nerves**, marrow, and fat, which rot away soon after the animal has died. If the bone is buried, these spaces may fill partly with sand or mud. Later on, the bone may be buried very deep, and waters containing minerals may pass through. Some of these minerals may also form inside the bone as crystals.

1. Dying
An animal falls to the bottom of the ocean when it dies. Scavenging animals may eat its flesh.

2. Rotting
Most of the flesh may be eaten, or it may rot away. Usually only the hard parts of the bony skeleton are left behind.

3. Buried
Over a relatively short time, mud and sand may be dumped on top of the skeleton, progressively burying it.

4. Fossil Skeleton
Millions of years later, the ancient sea-floor may have become dry land, and a paleontologist may find the skeleton.

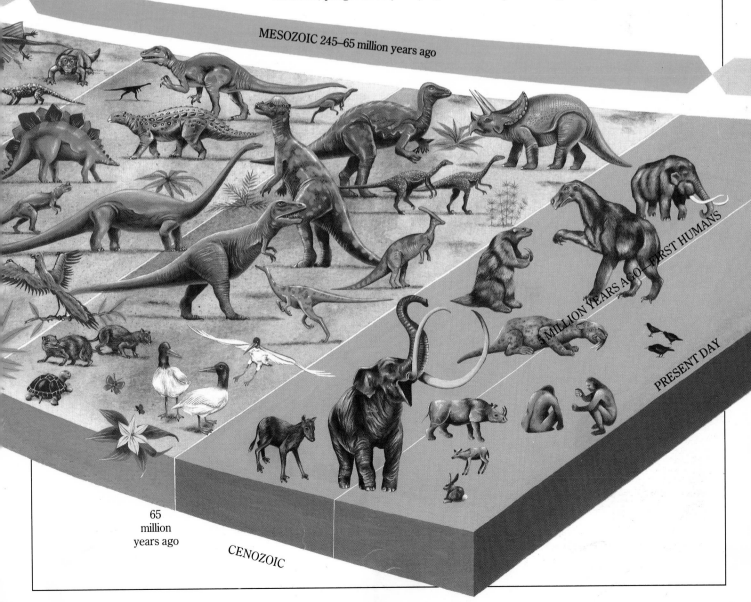

MESOZOIC 245–65 million years ago

1 MILLION YEARS AGO—FIRST HUMANS

PRESENT DAY

65 million years ago

CENOZOIC

17

Where They Came From?

Dinosaurs did not spring onto the Earth from nowhere. Nor were they the first and only great extinct animals of all time. A long history of the **evolution** of life is known before the dinosaurs came on the scene, indeed over 3 billion years of evolution! Dinosaurs are vertebrates, animals with backbones, just like us, and the first vertebrates were simple fishlike animals that lived about 500 million years ago. The first land vertebrates were **amphibians**, which came onto land about 375 million years ago. Then the reptiles appeared. It was about 225 million years ago that the first dinosaurs appeared.

EVOLUTION OF THE DINOSAURS

The oldest dinosaurs date from the Santa Maria Formation (shown on page 19), 225 million years ago. They were small, two-legged meat-eaters. The dinosaurs originated from among the archosaurs, a group that came to prominence during the Triassic Period and included some plant-eaters but mainly meat-eaters. Three or four main lines of dinosaur evolution became established during the late Triassic Period.

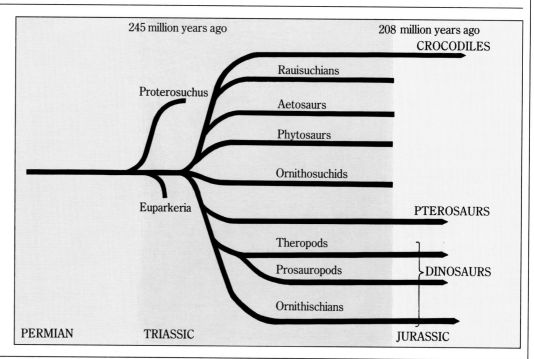

245 million years ago — 208 million years ago

CROCODILES
Rauisuchians
Proterosuchus
Aetosaurs
Phytosaurs
Ornithosuchids
Euparkeria
PTEROSAURS
Theropods
Prosauropods
DINOSAURS
Ornithischians

PERMIAN — TRIASSIC — JURASSIC

AGE OF MAMMALLIKE REPTILES

The first reptiles were small animals. They laid eggs on land and could live away from the water, unlike the amphibians, which laid their eggs in water. The first 100 million years of reptile evolution were dominated by the mammallike reptiles, small and large plant- and meat-eaters. These were true reptiles (they laid eggs and had scaly skins), but they had mammallike teeth. Reptiles have teeth that are all the same from the back to the front of the jaws, but mammals, and many mammallike reptiles, had different kinds of teeth. The mammallike reptiles were very successful.

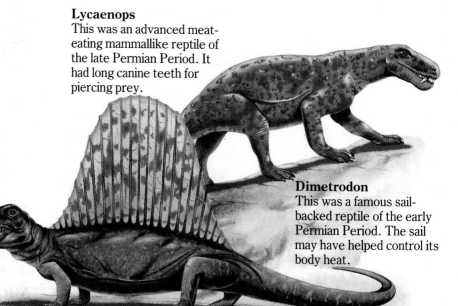

Lycaenops
This was an advanced meat-eating mammallike reptile of the late Permian Period. It had long canine teeth for piercing prey.

Dimetrodon
This was a famous sail-backed reptile of the early Permian Period. The sail may have helped control its body heat.

SANTA MARIA SITE

A fossil site in Brazil during the late Triassic Period, 225 million years ago, marks a turning point in the history of life on Earth. Most of the animals were mammallike reptiles, such as *Dinodontosaurus*, or other less familiar forms, such as *Scaphonyx*. A small two-legged meat-eater, *Herrerasaurus*, might not have seemed important. These animals were all over the world at the time. During the Triassic Period, all the continents were joined together, and the animals could move freely anywhere. Not long after, most of these creatures died out, and the dinosaurs took over.

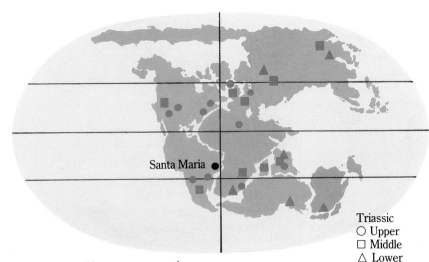

Santa Maria ●

Triassic
○ Upper
□ Middle
△ Lower

The world 225 million years ago, at the beginning of the Age of the Dinosaurs

1. Plant-eater
Scaphonyx was a plant-eating rhynchosaur ("snouted reptile")—an odd-looking animal, but the most common creature of its day.

2. The first dinosaur
Herrerasaurus, the first dinosaur, was rather rare. Only two or three skeletons are known, but it is the first dinosaur.

3. Mammallike reptile
Dinodontosaurus was one of the last of the mammallike reptiles.

But this was not the end of these reptiles. Distant relatives were slowly evolving into true mammals.

19

HOW DO WE KNOW
Where They Lived?

How do we know about the world of the dinosaurs? Did they live in steaming **tropical jungles**, or roasting sandy deserts? Are the scenes in books and movies accurate? The evidence comes from the rocks. Dinosaur bones are never found on their own. They are usually buried in sandstone or mudstone that tell a story to the geologists who study the sites. There may be evidence of an ancient river. There may be tree stumps, branches, and leaves that tell about the plants the dinosaurs may have fed on. There may be fossils of other animals— insects, fish, turtles, crocodiles—that complete the picture.

AN ANCIENT LANDSCAPE
The scene shown here is a detailed reconstruction of life during the early Cretaceous Period in southern England, 125 million years ago. It is based on dozens of dinosaur digs, over the past 150 years, in the Wealden rocks of Kent, Sussex, Surrey, and the Isle of Wight. Similar fossil sites have been found in other parts of the world, such as Montana and the Gobi Desert.

Plants
Leaves, stems, twigs, tree trunks, and roots show that there were all kinds of plants present, from waterside horsetails and ferns, to ginkgo, cycad, and conifer trees.

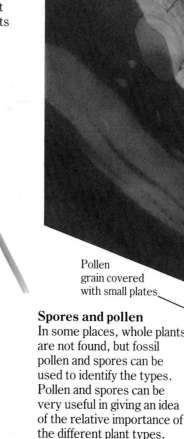

Fern frond

The hills were covered with conifer trees, ancestors of pines and spruces.

Dinosaurs like the plant-eater *Iguanodon* lived on the lowlands and fed on leaves from the trees.

Pollen grain covered with small plates

Spores and pollen
In some places, whole plants are not found, but fossil pollen and spores can be used to identify the types. Pollen and spores can be very useful in giving an idea of the relative importance of the different plant types.

Dinosaur bones may be found in river and lake sands and muds. The bones may be arranged as skeletons or washed downstream and scattered.

Fish
Various scaly fish lived in the ponds and rivers of the Wealden. Sometimes only scattered scales are found. In other cases whole masses of broken fish bones and, rarely, complete specimens are found.

Insects
Many kinds of insects buzzed over the ponds and rivers of the Wealden dinosaur lands, and others, such as cockroaches, beetles, bugs, and dragonflies, crept around in the leaves.

Sand and mud were washed down rivers from highlands around London.

Growth lines on clam shell

Tree trunks and other plant debris could wash down rivers and be dumped in great masses that have partly turned to coal.

Shells
Various kinds of small shells have been found in the Wealden. Some were pond snails and clams, and others were from swimming creatures. These show that it was warm.

The ancient lakes and river channels show up clearly in the rocks as long lens shapes.

What They Ate?

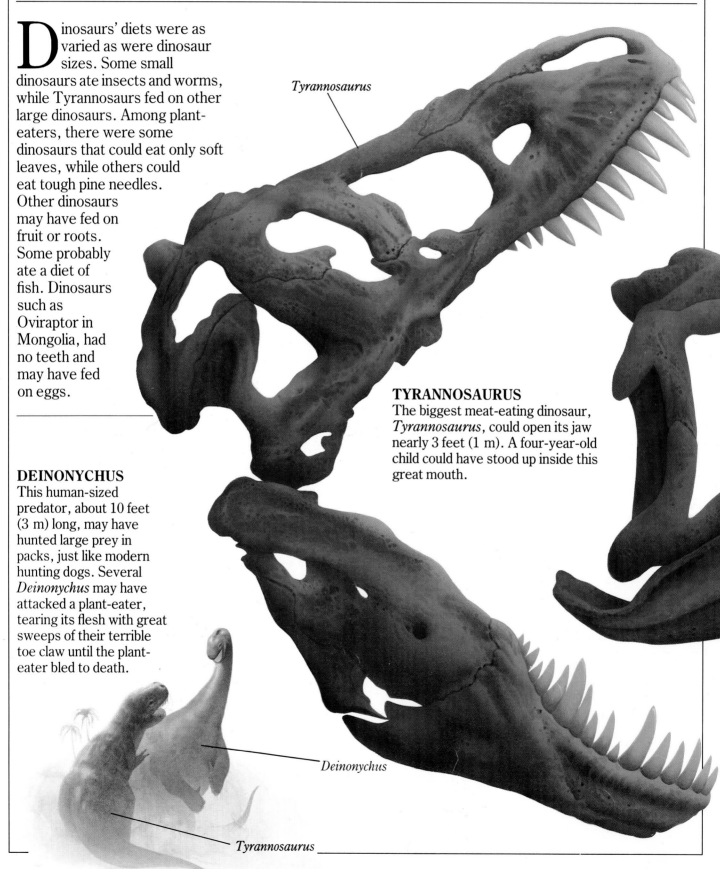

Dinosaurs' diets were as varied as were dinosaur sizes. Some small dinosaurs ate insects and worms, while Tyrannosaurs fed on other large dinosaurs. Among plant-eaters, there were some dinosaurs that could eat only soft leaves, while others could eat tough pine needles. Other dinosaurs may have fed on fruit or roots. Some probably ate a diet of fish. Dinosaurs such as Oviraptor in Mongolia, had no teeth and may have fed on eggs.

Tyrannosaurus

TYRANNOSAURUS

The biggest meat-eating dinosaur, *Tyrannosaurus*, could open its jaw nearly 3 feet (1 m). A four-year-old child could have stood up inside this great mouth.

DEINONYCHUS

This human-sized predator, about 10 feet (3 m) long, may have hunted large prey in packs, just like modern hunting dogs. Several *Deinonychus* may have attacked a plant-eater, tearing its flesh with great sweeps of their terrible toe claw until the plant-eater bled to death.

Deinonychus

Tyrannosaurus

22

PROBLEMS WITH PLANT-EATING

The most successful plant-eating dinosaurs were the ornithopods, two-legged dinosaurs, such as *Iguanodon* and the duckbills. They were even able to chew their food, something no other reptile can do. The ornithopods could not move their jaws around as we can. In some early forms (1), the lower jaws moved in as the jaws closed. In others (2), the sides of the skull flapped out as the jaws closed.

DIGESTIVE SYSTEM

Ornithopods could chew, and so their food was cut up a little. Other dinosaurs, like all reptiles living today, swallowed their food whole and might have had terrible indigestion. However, they probably had large muscular stomachs, which squeezed the food, and which contained acids to break it up. Plant-eating dinosaurs probably also swallowed sand or gravel to help grind their food.

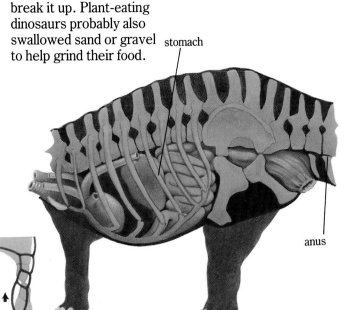
stomach

anus

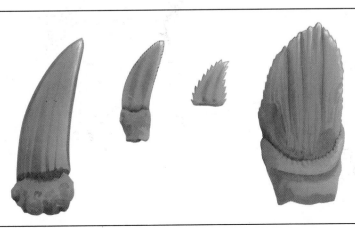

1

2

PLATEOSAURUS SKULL

The shape of this skull is quite different from the meat-eating *Tyrannosaurus* skull. The jaw joint, at the back, is set low, and the back part of the jaw is deep. Together, these show that there were powerful jaw muscles and a powerful bite near the back of the tooth row, both necessary for cutting tough plants. Stems and leaves could be gathered into the horselike skull and cut up along the length of the jaws.

Deinonychus

TEETH

Meat-eaters all have flattened, curved, pointed teeth with zigzag edges, all designed to saw up meat and bone. The teeth curve back in the jaws in order to keep the prey from escaping. Plant-eating dinosaurs had a variety of "leaf-shaped" teeth, usually quite broad and flat, often ridged, and often with coarse, zigzag edges.

If Dinosaurs Slept?

Did dinosaurs sleep, like dogs, cats, and humans, or were they awake all the time, like many animals? Did dinosaurs go out to feed during the day or at night? Were they **warm-blooded** or not? These are some of the most difficult questions to answer, since it is hard to know how to begin to find out. However, paleontologists can make some sensible guesses based on modern animals. And, there are a surprising number of ways of looking at the question of body temperature.

Kamptobaatar
Early mammals, such as *Kamptobaatar*, lived side by side with the dinosaurs. In fact, mammals had arisen not long after the dinosaurs (see page 17). They had hair, were warm-blooded, and probably fed at night.

Tarbosaurus
The great dinosaurs, such as *Tarbosaurus*, probably slept at night. It may not have been the deep sleep that humans need, but the sleep of a cold-blooded animal. As the air became colder, the large dinosaurs may simply have slowed down.

BODY TEMPERATURE

Cold-blooded animals, such as lizards and snakes, are not always cold. Their body temperature is usually the same as the air temperature, so they can be very hot on a hot day! Warm-blooded animals, such as humans, keep the same body temperature all the time, whether the air is hot or cold. Large, cold-blooded animals (like big crocodiles) are somewhere in between. They take so long to warm up and so long to cool down that their body temperature actually stays fairly constant, even when nights are cold and days are very hot.

BONE STRUCTURE

In 1975, several paleontologists noticed that dinosaur bone looked very much like mammal bone when it was cut into slices and examined under the microscope. It did not seem to be anything like the bone structure of a cold-blooded lizard. It turns out, however, that all large animals have the "mammal" type of bone, and small animals have the "lizard" type.

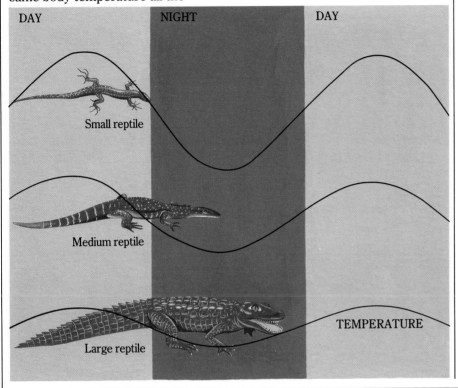

Small reptile

Medium reptile

Large reptile

DAY   NIGHT   DAY

TEMPERATURE

Lizard bone

Dinosaur bone

Blood vessel canal

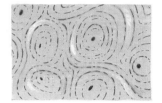

Cow bone

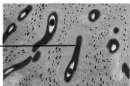

Stegosaurus

This plated dinosaur gives clues about dinosaur body heat. What were the great plates for along the middle of the back of *Stegosaurus*? They stood up too high to be much use in protecting the body from meat-eaters. They were covered with blood vessels and must have worked like radiators. Experiments with a metal *Stegosaurus* in a wind tunnel showed how the plates were perfect for taking in and giving off heat.

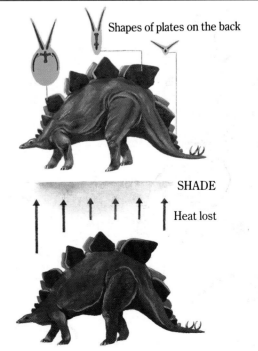

Shapes of plates on the back

SHADE

Heat lost

SUN

Heat taken in

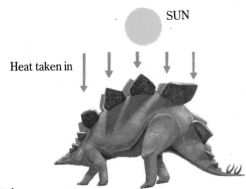

Heating
Early in the morning, *Stegosaurus* could stand sideways to the sun, and heat would be absorbed through the plates and passed into the body through the **bloodstream**.

Cooling
Later on, when the afternoon sun became too hot, *Stegosaurus* could find some shade or stand in a breeze, and heat would have been radiated from the plates.

HOW DO WE KNOW
If They Could Run?

How fast could the fastest dinosaur run? How can we measure dinosaur speeds? A great deal can be learned about dinosaurs walking and running from the bones of the legs. The joints can be examined to see just how the legs could move. The leg muscles can be restored, layer by layer, and even the strengths of those muscles can be calculated (the fatter a muscle is, the stronger it is). The shape of a dinosaur's leg bones and muscles can be compared with modern animals, such as horses, humans, rhinos, elephants, and ostriches, to find how that dinosaur could run. Most amazingly, recent studies of dinosaur footprints have shown that they can give exact readings of running speeds.

FAST AND SLOW

The slowest dinosaurs moved at 1 mile per hour (1–2 kph) or less, which is slower than human walking speed. Most of them seem to have walked at about the speed of a grown human who is in a hurry, which is about 3–4 miles per hour (5–6 kph).

Running styles

The running styles of an ostrich dinosaur is based on movies of a modern ostrich moving. An ostrich is a flightless bird with the same build as an ostrich dinosaur. It could run at the same speed as a galloping horse.

TRACKS

Fossil dinosaur footprints and pathways are very common in all parts of the world. They used to be seen as just another interesting piece of evidence for the shape of dinosaurs' feet. Footprints can show the exact shape of the flesh of the foot, claws, and even skin patterns. They also tell us how fast dinosaurs were. A simple equation, worked out in 1976, shows that the speed is in proportion to the stride length (the spacing of the footprints).

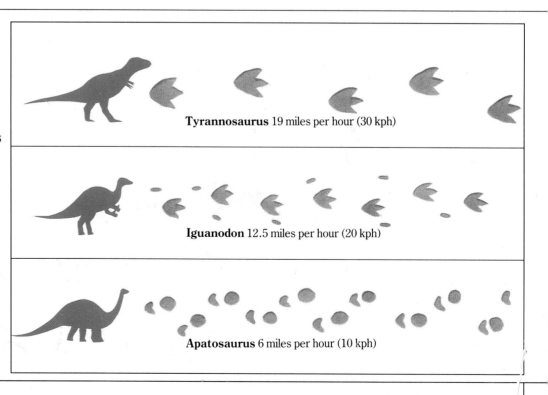

Tyrannosaurus 19 miles per hour (30 kph)

Iguanodon 12.5 miles per hour (20 kph)

Apatosaurus 6 miles per hour (10 kph)

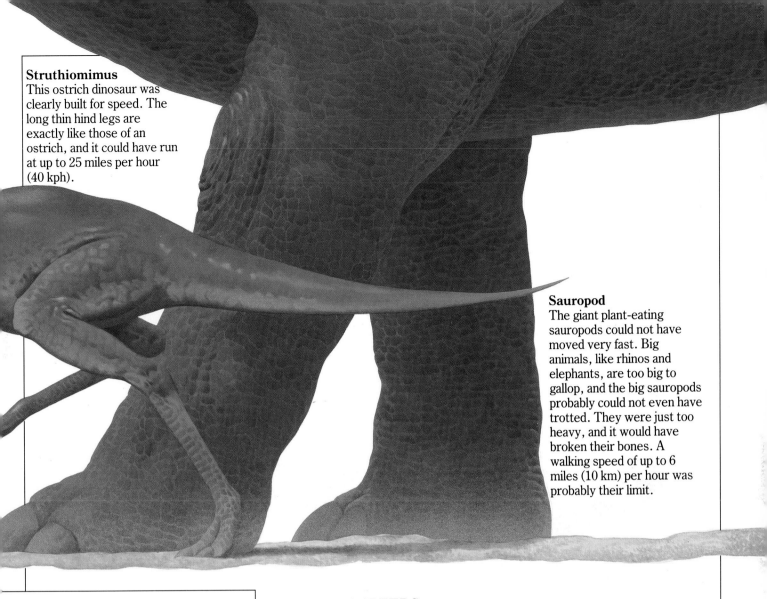

Struthiomimus
This ostrich dinosaur was clearly built for speed. The long thin hind legs are exactly like those of an ostrich, and it could have run at up to 25 miles per hour (40 kph).

Sauropod
The giant plant-eating sauropods could not have moved very fast. Big animals, like rhinos and elephants, are too big to gallop, and the big sauropods probably could not even have trotted. They were just too heavy, and it would have broken their bones. A walking speed of up to 6 miles (10 km) per hour was probably their limit.

Modern comparisons
Tracks of modern animals have helped paleontologists study dinosaur tracks, revealing how dinosaurs walked and ran.

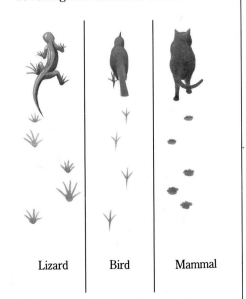

| Lizard | Bird | Mammal |

COMPARING SPEEDS

Large heavy animals can only walk. Slightly smaller animals, like rhinos, can trot, which is just a kind of fast walking. Medium-sized animals, such as horses and dogs, can gallop, which is a very fast run. Fastest of all are cheetahs, which can reach speeds of 70 miles per hour (112 kph). There were probably no dinosaurs as fast as that!

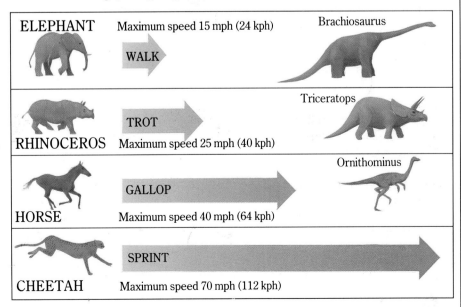

ELEPHANT Maximum speed 15 mph (24 kph) WALK Brachiosaurus

RHINOCEROS TROT Maximum speed 25 mph (40 kph) Triceratops

HORSE GALLOP Maximum speed 40 mph (64 kph) Ornithominus

CHEETAH SPRINT Maximum speed 70 mph (112 kph)

HOW DO WE KNOW
If They Could Swim?

Most animals can swim, even if some, like cats, do not like it! At one time, paleontologists thought that only the large sauropods could swim and that duckbilled dinosaurs could swim using a kind of built-in **snorkel**. They believed that these plant-eaters stayed in the middle of lakes to escape from meat-eating dinosaurs. There are many reasons why these ideas are wrong. There is proof that the meat-eaters could swim. The sauropods would have died if they had lived in deep lakes, and duckbills did not have snorkels, but they did have trumpetlike chests (see page 31).

OLD AND NEW VIEWS

The large plant-eating sauropods certainly lived near lakes some of the time. But it is very unlikely that they stood in the middle of deep lakes, using their long necks to detect danger. A scientific experiment shows why. As the water becomes deeper, the pressure increases, and it is harder to breathe. Below 6.5–10 feet (2–3 m) deep, the sauropod could not inhale.

Wrong View
A sauropod living in a deep lake

The experiment
You can breathe through a 12-inch- (30-cm-) long snorkel. It is hard to breathe through a 3-foot (1-m) snorkel, and impossible through a 6.5-foot - (2-m-) long one.

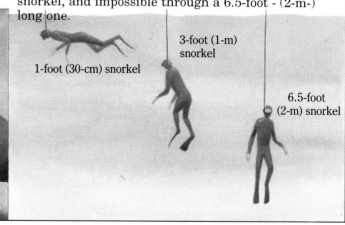

1-foot (30-cm) snorkel

3-foot (1-m) snorkel

6.5-foot (2-m) snorkel

COULD MEAT-EATERS SWIM?

The old idea was that a fierce meat-eating dinosaur would chase a herd of plant-eaters down to the waterside. The plant-eaters would jump in and swim away to safety, and the meat-eater would be left on the bank growling and snarling in rage. This is not true, of course, and the evidence to prove it wrong, the tracks of a swimming *Megalosaurus*, was found in the 1980s.

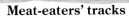

Meat-eaters' tracks

The tracks above showed that meat-eaters could swim. While its body floated, *Megalosaurus* moved itself along with delicate kicks on the bottom of an ancient lake.

SAUROPOD SWIMMING

The great sauropods could swim as well as any other dinosaur, but they did it with their necks stretched out straight in front. In this position, the lungs (inside the chest) were just below the surface, and the dinosaur could breathe easily. Some fossil tracks show the sauropods padding themselves along in the water with just their feet touching the bottom.

If Dinosaurs Could Think?

Dinosaurs are often said to have been very stupid. They were huge but had tiny brains. This means that they could not have thought about very much and is often suggested as the reason why they died out. Of course, when paleontologists look more closely at the evidence, by studying the sizes of dinosaurs' brains, the story is not so simple. In fact, most dinosaurs were just as intelligent, or just as stupid, as modern reptiles. Some dinosaurs were actually as clever as birds.

BRAINS

Dinosaur brains can sometimes be studied in detail. The brain fitted tightly into a space in the back of the skull, and the bones that wrapped around the brain to protect it show its exact shape. It is possible to look at a cast from the inside of the braincase and determine the exact shape of the dinosaur's brain.

Brain cast

This brain cast from *Tyrannosaurus* (above) is a long, sausage-shaped object, really very small compared to the size of the animal. The lumps and blobs in the brain are the different parts, connected with hearing, sight, smell, balance, and so on. Many nerves pass out of the side of the brain and help to operate the mouth, the eyes, the ears, and other parts.

Braincase

Saurornithoides had a bird-sized brain. This intelligent dinosaur had a large braincase, and its brain was much larger in proportion to its body size than the brain of most dinosaurs. The biggest parts of the brain were for vision and for balance, which indicates that *Saurornithoides* led a very active life.

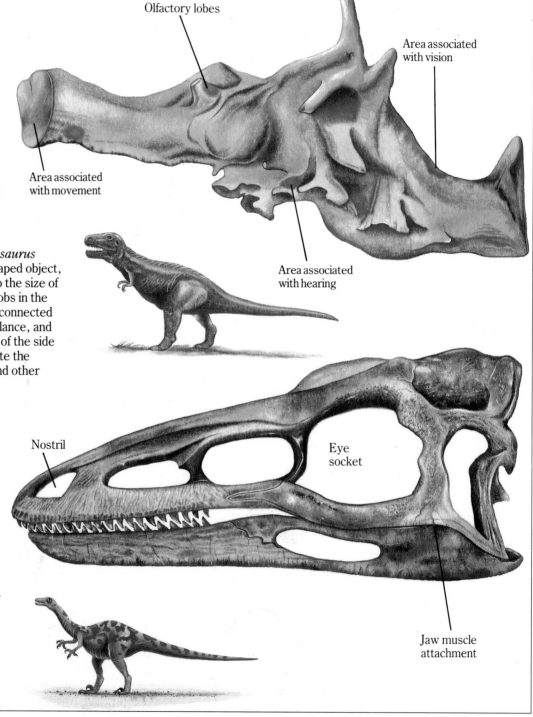

Olfactory lobes

Area associated with vision

Area associated with movement

Area associated with hearing

Nostril

Eye socket

Jaw muscle attachment

COMPARING BRAIN SIZES

Weight for weight, mammals, such as humans, have larger brains than birds, and birds have larger brains than reptiles and most dinosaurs. The important thing is to remember that actual brain size is not an accurate guide to intelligence. After all, elephants have bigger brains than humans. What is important is the relative brain size, in proportion to body size. Humans have very high relative brain sizes, while dinosaurs have very small relative brain sizes.

Dinosaur
The dinosaur brain is relatively small and only fills a very small part of the skull at the back.

Mammal
The mammal brain is relatively large and fills up a large part of the inside of the skull.

Reptile
The reptile brain, in a modern lizard, snake, crocodile, or turtle, is quite small, just as in most dinosaurs.

Bird
Birds have relatively large brains, which fill up a great deal of the skull, just as in mammals.

ADAPTING

One scientist thought that dinosaurs were so stupid that they could not have learned from their mistakes. They would keep on banging their heads on branches, falling over stones, and eating poisonous plants. This is not likely, however. Dinosaurs were very successful animals, and they were no more stupid than a living crocodile.

DUCKBILLS

Evidence that dinosaurs were not all stupid comes from the duckbills. They could tell each other apart by looking at faces, just as humans do. They could do this also by listening to each other's voices. The crests on top of the duckbills' heads were different in males and females, and different in their young. Also, each species had a different crest.

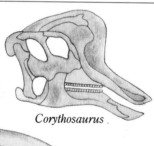
Corythosaurus

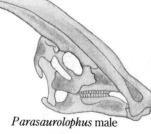
Parasaurolophus male

Parasaurolophus female

A hollow crest
The crest was hollow and carried the breathing tubes inside. When it breathed out, the duckbill made a great honking noise. Different-shaped crests made different honks, so every dinosaur had a different voice.

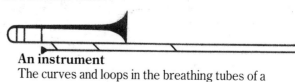

An instrument
The curves and loops in the breathing tubes of a duckbill are similar to the curves in a trombone.

An orchestra!
Different instruments sound different. Experiments with duckbill skulls sound like an ancient orchestra!

How Dinosaurs Bred?

Reptiles lay eggs, just as birds do. However, modern reptiles usually lay their eggs on the ground, or bury them in sand. Dinosaurs also laid eggs, and dinosaur nests have been known for some time. The first dinosaur nests were found around 1925 in Mongolia. But it is only recently that paleontologists have studied dinosaur nests in detail. It turns out that dinosaurs may even have sat on their nests and protected the eggs. They also helped the newborn babies by bringing them food. As far as we can tell, dinosaurs were good parents.

SIZE OF EGGS

Many dinosaurs were huge, and it might seem logical that they must have laid huge eggs. This is not the case, however. The biggest dinosaur eggs were about 1 foot (30 cm) long, the same size as the biggest birds' eggs. The reason that big dinosaurs did not lay huge eggs is that the young had to be able to get out. The bigger an egg is, the thicker its shell has to be, or it might collapse. If the shell is too thick, the baby cannot get out.

Ostrich
The biggest eggs today are laid by ostriches. Extinct flightless birds laid even larger ones, up to 1 foot (30 cm) long.

Turkey
Turkeys lay medium-sized eggs relative to their body size. They are much bigger than a common hen's egg.

Hen
A hen's egg is still larger than the eggs of many smaller birds and reptiles.

DINOSAUR NESTS

Dinosaur nests in Montana show that dinosaur mothers came back year after year to the same nesting site. Paleontologists have dug down through layers of rock and have found dinosaur nests one on top of the other. The nests were dug out each year then covered by floodwaters carrying sand and mud, and then new nests were dug on top the following year.

Sites
This diagram shows layers of rock separated to show the nest sites in similar places year after year.

DINOSAUR EGGS

Inside the egg, the embryo gets larger until it is big enough to hatch. The embryo feeds on a special high-protein food that is inside the yolk, and there is even a special bag for waste products.

Fossil egg
Dinosaur eggs were covered with a hard shell, like the shell of a hen's egg. In dinosaurs, this shell often had a rough pattern on the outside. Fossil specimens were often found crushed.

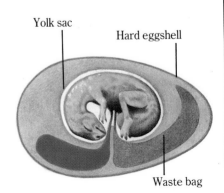

Yolk sac

Hard eggshell

Waste bag

HOW DINOSAURS MADE NESTS

The dinosaur nests in Montana have shown in some detail how dinosaurs built their nests. The nests were made by a duckbilled dinosaur called *Maiasaura* ("good mother reptile") and a plant-eating relative of *Hypsilophodon* called *Orodromeus*. Hundreds of nests have been found at a site that has been renamed "Egg Mountain."

The favorite nesting site seems to have been on an island. The site is surrounded by rocks laid down in lake waters, and it rises above these layers. Perhaps this site was safer for the nests, away from some of the animals that might have tried to eat the eggs.

Hatching
Babies hatched out of their eggs when they were ready to feed. A special tooth helped them break the shell.

1. First, the mother dinosaur found a dry patch of ground, and she built a low mound with a broad hollow area in the middle. She used her front feet to do this.

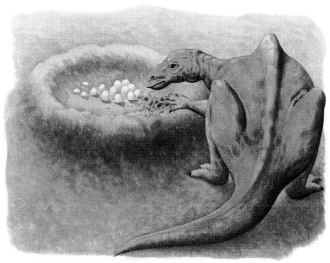

2. Then she laid her eggs in the hollow, arranging them in careful circles and burying the bottom part of each egg in the earth so they did not roll around.

3. She covered the eggs with some light soil and large rotting leaves. This formed a kind of compost on top that helped to keep the eggs warm.

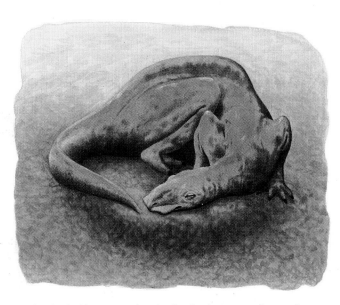

4. As the babies were developing in the eggs, the mother may have sat on the nest mound, partly to keep the eggs warm and partly to protect them from egg-eating animals.

About Flying Reptiles?

People think that dinosaurs could not fly. But, the most successful dinosaurs of all time could fly. What does this mean? Some of the small two-legged meat-eating dinosaurs evolved into birds about 150 million years ago. So, birds developed from dinosaurs, which in a way means that birds are very successful living dinosaurs.

The most successful flyers in the age of the dinosaurs were the pterosaurs, "winged reptiles,"

which lived during the same period as the dinosaurs, from 225 million years ago until the great extinction, 65 million years ago. The pterosaurs included the largest flying animals of all time, some as large as light aircraft.

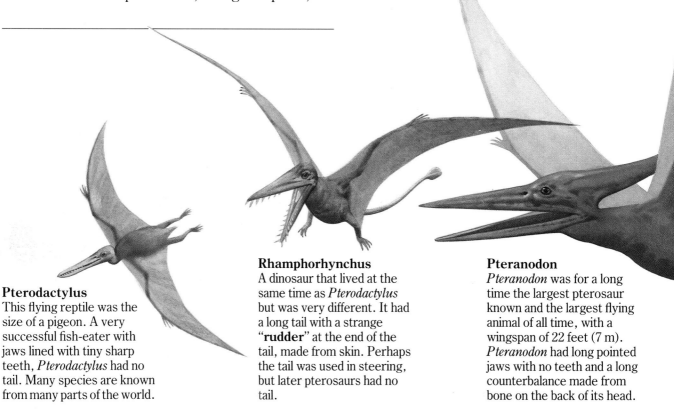

Pterodactylus
This flying reptile was the size of a pigeon. A very successful fish-eater with jaws lined with tiny sharp teeth, *Pterodactylus* had no tail. Many species are known from many parts of the world.

Rhamphorhynchus
A dinosaur that lived at the same time as *Pterodactylus* but was very different. It had a long tail with a strange "**rudder**" at the end of the tail, made from skin. Perhaps the tail was used in steering, but later pterosaurs had no tail.

Pteranodon
Pteranodon was for a long time the largest pterosaur known and the largest flying animal of all time, with a wingspan of 22 feet (7 m). *Pteranodon* had long pointed jaws with no teeth and a long counterbalance made from bone on the back of its head.

FLIGHT PATTERNS

Pterosaurs could fly, or they would not have had wings. But the very large ones must have had problems in flapping such huge wings. They probably flew by using currents of warm air that rise from the surface of the Earth. This would allow them to soar.

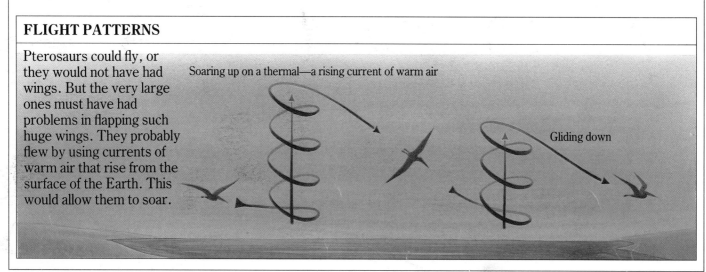

Soaring up on a thermal—a rising current of warm air

Gliding down

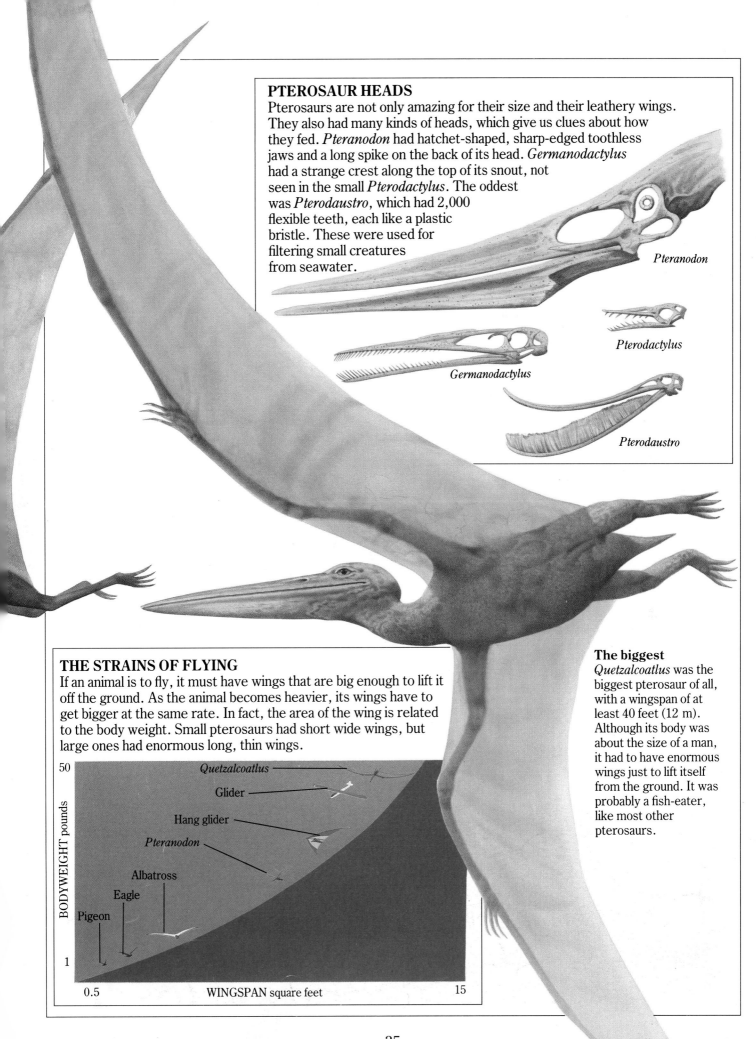

PTEROSAUR HEADS

Pterosaurs are not only amazing for their size and their leathery wings. They also had many kinds of heads, which give us clues about how they fed. *Pteranodon* had hatchet-shaped, sharp-edged toothless jaws and a long spike on the back of its head. *Germanodactylus* had a strange crest along the top of its snout, not seen in the small *Pterodactylus*. The oddest was *Pterodaustro*, which had 2,000 flexible teeth, each like a plastic bristle. These were used for filtering small creatures from seawater.

Pteranodon

Pterodactylus

Germanodactylus

Pterodaustro

THE STRAINS OF FLYING

If an animal is to fly, it must have wings that are big enough to lift it off the ground. As the animal becomes heavier, its wings have to get bigger at the same rate. In fact, the area of the wing is related to the body weight. Small pterosaurs had short wide wings, but large ones had enormous long, thin wings.

BODYWEIGHT pounds

50

Quetzalcoatlus

Glider

Hang glider

Pteranodon

Albatross

Eagle

Pigeon

1

0.5   WINGSPAN square feet   15

The biggest

Quetzalcoatlus was the biggest pterosaur of all, with a wingspan of at least 40 feet (12 m). Although its body was about the size of a man, it had to have enormous wings just to lift itself from the ground. It was probably a fish-eater, like most other pterosaurs.

Who Ruled the Ocean?

D inosaurs could swim and often did. But the rulers of the oceans were two other groups of extinct reptiles, the ichthyosaurs and the plesiosaurs. Both groups arose some time before the dinosaurs, and the plesiosaurs lived at least to the end of the age of the dinosaurs, 65 million years ago. The ichthyosaurs seem to have died out about 90 million years ago. Both groups were hugely successful in the ocean, and yet they arose from animals that lived on land.

Ichthyosaurus
A dolphin-shaped animal, 9 to 12 feet (3 to 4 m) long. Its front and back feet had become paddles, and it had a tail fin and a sharklike fin in the middle of its back. Ichthyosaurs produced live young in the water, just as whales and dolphins do today.

ICHTHYOSAUR DIET

Skull
The skull has long jaws lined with many sharp pointed teeth. The jaws were used to snap up fish and shellfish.

Food
Fossilized stomach contents contain the remains of thousands of shellfish.

Dung
Fossilized dung is often full of fish bones and scales.

Pliosaurus
This is a special kind of plesiosaur called a pliosaur. It has a massive skull and a short neck, and probably fed on other smaller sea reptiles like ichthyosaurs.

Elasmosaurus
A remarkable long-necked plesiosaur. It had 40 or more bones in its neck, and it is likely that it could bend its neck around like a snake in order to catch fast-moving fish.

EVOLUTION

The sea reptiles evolved from animals that lived on land, but the early stages in their evolution are not clear. Certainly the oldest ichthyosaurs and plesiosaurs did not have paddles, but still had the feet of land animals. There were many other sea reptiles, such as shell-eating placodonts, giant mosasaurs, sea crocodiles, and even seabirds later on.

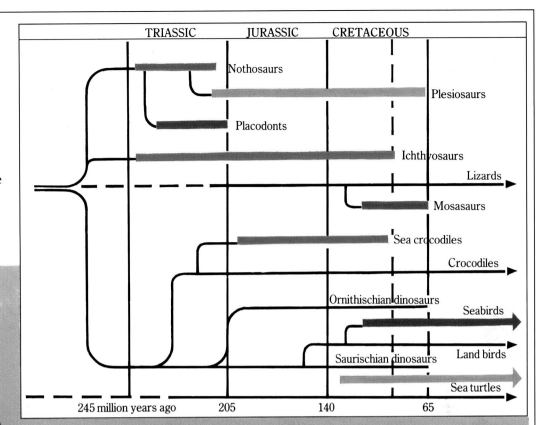

	TRIASSIC	JURASSIC	CRETACEOUS

Nothosaurs

Plesiosaurs

Placodonts

Ichthyosaurs

Lizards

Mosasaurs

Sea crocodiles

Crocodiles

Ornithischian dinosaurs

Seabirds

Land birds

Saurischian dinosaurs

Sea turtles

245 million years ago   205   140   65

TYPES OF SWIMMING

Some animals use their whole bodies for swimming by throwing themselves into great curves. Some beat their tail from side to side or up and down, while others "fly" underwater, using their paddles. Some even row.

Body undulation

Tail beating

Underwater flying

Rowing

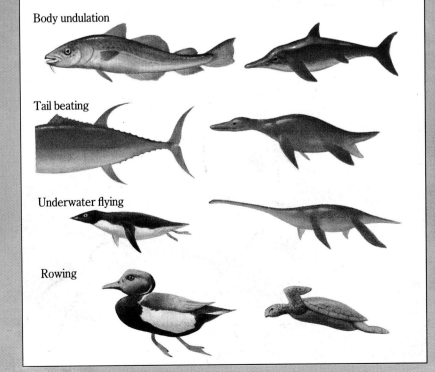

What Killed the Dinosaurs?

T he dinosaurs, and many other kinds of plants and animals, died out 65 million years ago. It seems that this mass extinction happened quite rapidly, and it is a fascinating mystery to try to find out just what happened. Many scientists now think that a giant meteorite, an **asteroid**, hit the Earth at that time, while others think that the climates were changing in a gradual way. No single theory can explain everything that happened so many years ago.

THE ASTEROID THEORY

The idea is that an asteroid, 6 miles (10 km) across, hit the Earth and exploded. This would have sent a huge cloud of dust and rocks into the sky, which would have blacked out the sun. Without sunlight, temperatures would fall, and plants and animals would die. The dust later fell to Earth and has been found at locations all over the world.

Dust layer

The "dinosaur death dust layer" has been found in over 100 places around the world, in rocks that are exactly 65 million years old. Could it have come from a volcano? A site in Australia has been identified as a source of the volcanic dust.

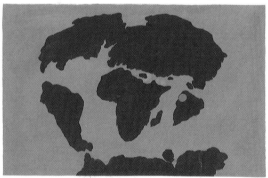

Site of volcano

What lived and what died?	
Died	**Lived**
Dinosaurs	Crocodiles
Pterosaurs	Birds
Plesiosaurs	Turtles
Mosasaurs	Lizards and snakes
Ammonites	Mammals
Belemnites	Fish
Rudist bivalves	Insects
Foraminifera	Plants
	Most shellfish

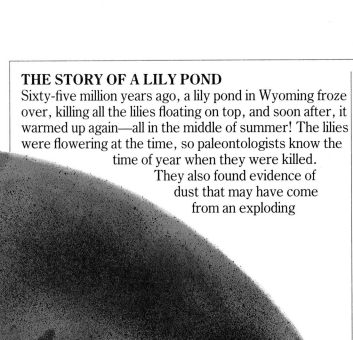

THE STORY OF A LILY POND

Sixty-five million years ago, a lily pond in Wyoming froze over, killing all the lilies floating on top, and soon after, it warmed up again—all in the middle of summer! The lilies were flowering at the time, so paleontologists know the time of year when they were killed. They also found evidence of dust that may have come from an exploding asteroid (because iridium, common in asteroids was found in the pond) or from a huge volcanic eruption.

The occurrence of debris shows that either volcanic dust or asteroid material landed in the pond, lowering the temperature and so killing the lilies. This could have been what happened to the dinosaurs.

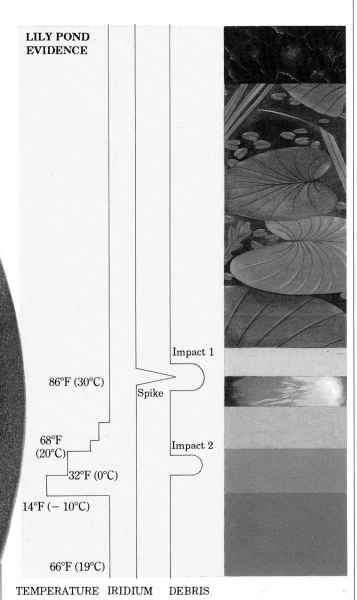

LILY POND EVIDENCE

86°F (30°C)

Spike

Impact 1

68°F (20°C)

Impact 2

32°F (0°C)

14°F (− 10°C)

66°F (19°C)

TEMPERATURE   IRIDIUM   DEBRIS

VICTIMS AND SURVIVORS

The key to the mystery of the great extinction may be found in the end by looking at which plants and animals died and which survived. Any theory has to be able to explain why dinosaurs and the great sea reptiles perished, but crocodiles, turtles, lizards, snakes, birds, and mammals survived. Why did some groups of shellfish die out and others not? No single acceptable theory answers the question of why dinosaurs became extinct.

Glossary

Amphibian
A land animal, like a frog or salamander, that has to lay its eggs in water

Ancestor
A plant or animal that gave rise to another or to a whole group

Asteroid
A large meteorite; a mass of rock in space that may hit planets, like the Earth

Bloodstream
The flow of blood in vessels throughout the body, from the heart to the lungs to the rest of the body

Cold-blooded
Animals, such as fish and reptiles, whose body temperatures depend on the temperature of their surroundings

Evolution
The ways in which plants and animals have changed or adapted themselves from one form into another through time

Gulley
A deep channel worn in sediment by heavy rain and rapid drainage

Mummified
Dried out animal or human remains, where skin and other "soft" parts may be preserved as well as the bone

Nerves
Special cells in the body that carry messages from the brain to the muscles or sense organs (eyes, ears, nose, tongue) and back again

Porous
Containing holes or spaces

Predator
A meat-eater; an animal that eats other animals, its prey

Quarry
A hole in the ground that has been dug or blasted with explosives in order to take out rock or gravel for making buildings or roads

Radioactive elements
Substances that change into other substances, and give off high-energy rays while doing so

Rudder
A board fixed to the back of a boat, used in steering

Snorkel
A breathing tube used by divers and other swimmers to allow them to breath underwater

Specimen
An example of a fossil or a rock

Three-dimensional
Solid, not flat like a printed page, which is two-dimensional

Tropical jungle
Large trees and plants that grow and live in hot damp parts of the world

Warm-blooded
Animals, such as birds and mammals, that have constant body temperatures

Index